Adapted by **David Lewman**

Illustrated by **Megan Fisher**

Published in the United States by Golden Books, an imprint of Random House Children's Books,
a division of Penguin Random House LLC, 1745 Broadway, New York, NY 10019, and in Canada by Penguin
Random House Canada Limited, Toronto. Golden Books, A Golden Book, A Big Golden Book, the G colophon,
and the distinctive gold spine are registered trademarks of Penguin Random House LLC. Nickelodeon,
Nick Jr., Sunny Day, and all related titles, logos, and characters are trademarks of Viacom International Inc.
rhcbooks.com
ISBN 978-1-5247-6876-8
Printed in the United States of America
10 9 8 7 6 5 4 3 2 1

Sunny Day

Puppy Love!

 A GOLDEN BOOK · NEW YORK

*O*ne day, Sunny, Rox, and Blair were sorting colorful wigs in their salon. They realized they needed more wig stands. Eager to help, Doodle dashed out the door to get some from the Glam Van.

On his way there, he noticed a cute little puppy. She was all alone.

"Aww," Doodle said. "I'm going to call you Fluffy. You can live with me and be *my* puppy!"

Back in the salon, Sunny said, "She's very cute, Doodle, but we can't keep her. She probably belongs to someone."

"I didn't think of that," Doodle admitted. "They must miss her very much!"

Just then, Scratch the dogcatcher came into the salon carrying a cage. Doodle quickly hid Fluffy under a wig.

"I'm looking for a puppy," said Scratch.

"This is a hair salon," Sunny said innocently. "You should try the pet store!"

But Scratch was suspicious. He searched the salon. The girls kept moving Fluffy to keep her out of Scratch's sight.

"Looks like we're a puppy-free zone!" Sunny said, steering Scratch to the door.

As soon as he stepped outside, Sunny quickly flipped the door sign to CLOSED. "We have to find Fluffy's owner," she said, "and fast!"

Sunny and her friends got into
the Glam Van and headed out to find
Fluffy's owner.

"Ready, set, gear up, and go!" they cheered.
But as they drove away, Fluffy stuck her head out
the window and barked.

Yip!

Scratch heard the bark! He ran to his truck to chase after
the Glam Van.

Sunny and her friends sped to Cindy's Bakery
to ask Cindy if she knew who Fluffy's owner was.
"Sorry, I don't," she said, scratching Fluffy
behind an ear.
Then Blair spotted Scratch outside the bakery!
"Cindy, can we leave through the back door?"
Sunny asked.
"Right this way!" she said, leading them out.

They hurried over to Peter's Flower Shop, but Peter didn't know who owned Fluffy, either.

Suddenly, Scratch came into the shop! Doodle hid Fluffy under a flowerpot. Scratch searched under the pots, but the puppy was quick—she dashed behind tulips before he could see her.

Sunny grabbed Fluffy and hid her in a pocket of her accessory apron.

"Time to go!" she said, hurrying out.

Scratch left Peter's Flower Shop and headed back to his truck. The Glam Van drove by. Fluffy looked out the van window and barked.

Yip!

Scratch stamped his feet. He jumped into his truck to follow the girls!

Next stop: Lacey's house. Lacey came to
the front door with her dog, KC. She was
scowling—until she saw Fluffy.

"Puppy!" she squealed. "So fluffy and cute!
I want her!"

"Do you know who her owner is?" Rox asked.

"No," Lacey said. "But finders keepers!"
She grabbed Fluffy out of Sunny's arms and
slammed the door!

Inside, Lacey gave the puppy some of KC's blankets and toys.

"*My* blankets?" KC exclaimed. He couldn't believe what was happening. "*My* toys?"

"And I'll get some of KC's doggie treats for you, too," Lacey said to the puppy.

"Unacceptable!" KC fumed.

In the backyard, Sunny dug through her accessory apron.

"Hair ribbons, curlers, sticky wax . . ." Then she grabbed a bucket off the ground.

"We're going puppy fishing!" Sunny explained.

She stuck the curlers together with the wax, then tied a string of ribbons to the end to make a fishing rod and line. At the end of the line, she fastened the bucket and tossed in one of Doodle's biscuits. Finally, she cast the bucket into the air and down through a skylight into Lacey's house!

Scratch spotted the Glam Van outside Lacey's house. He screeched his truck to a stop, got out, and rang the doorbell. Lacey peeked through the window at the dogcatcher.

"No one's here right now," she said. "But if you have a gift, please leave it outside. Bye-bye!"

Scratch rang the bell again. This time, KC stuck his head out the doggie door. Eager to get rid of Fluffy, he opened the door for Scratch. "Come right this way!" he said.

Meanwhile, Sunny's bucket was lowered into the living room. Fluffy jumped in and grabbed the biscuit. Sunny immediately pulled the bucket up toward the skylight.

KC and Scratch entered the living room just then—but they were too late. Little Fluffy was already out of the house and safe in Sunny's arms!

Lacey came in, saw Scratch, and quickly ushered him out the front door. Again Scratch heard a familiar bark.

Yip! Yip!

He saw Fluffy riding in the Glam Van with Sunny and her friends! Scratch darted to his truck, hopped in, and raced off.

Lacey looked down at KC. "Guess you're top dog again."

KC grinned happily.

In the Glam Van, the girls were working on their plan to find Fluffy's owner. Then Doodle noticed that Fluffy was missing!

Sunny pulled over. She and her friends looked everywhere for the frisky little pup. Suddenly, Fluffy leaped out from where she'd been hiding and jumped from the van!

Rox tossed down her skateboard, zoomed after Fluffy, and scooped her up.

Scratch spotted Sunny, Blair, Rox, and the dogs as they ran into an arcade. He dashed in after them, but they had already found good hiding places.

The girls and dogs ducked into a pile of stuffed animals. Then Fluffy ran away to hide in a game.

They managed to slip away without being seen by the dogcatcher.

Whew!

Outside the arcade, Doodle and Fluffy hid in a pedal cart, but Scratch saw them again!

He ran over. "Give me that puppy!" he said, out of breath.

Fluffy jumped up and down in the cart excitedly—causing it to roll down a hill!

"Sunny!" Doodle cried. "I don't know how to stop it!"

Sunny, Blair, and Rox jumped back into the Glam Van and chased after the runaway cart.

"Grab some ribbons, bands—anything we can knot together to make a lasso!" Sunny told her friends.

They were catching up to the rolling cart . . . but it was headed straight for the ocean!

Sunny tossed her lasso and stopped the cart before it plunged into the water! The girls ran to the dogs—and so did Scratch!

Oh, no! thought Sunny. There was no way for Fluffy to escape now. But Fluffy didn't run. The little dog jumped into Scratch's arms!

"Looks like she really likes you," Sunny said, confused.

"I know," Scratch said. "I'm her owner!"

"Owner?" the friends said at the same time.

Scratch told them the dog's name was Posey. "And I'm going to make her my assistant!" he said. "She knows every hiding place for runaway dogs, so no one would do a better job."

"Hmm," Sunny said, getting an idea. "If she's going to be your assistant, she really needs to look the part!"

With Doodle's help . . .

Sunny styled Posey's hair . . .

so it looked just like Scratch's!

"Thanks, Sunny!" the dogcatcher said. "And, Doodle, you can visit Posey anytime."

After they left, Doodle told Sunny, "Between you and me, I think I'm happier being *your* dog than having one of my own!"